Dunc and the Scam Artists

OTHER YEARLING BOOKS YOU WILL ENJOY:

THE COOKCAMP, *Gary Paulsen*
THE VOYAGE OF THE *FROG*, *Gary Paulsen*
THE BOY WHO OWNED THE SCHOOL, *Gary Paulsen*
HOW TO EAT FRIED WORMS, *Thomas Rockwell*
HOW TO FIGHT A GIRL, *Thomas Rockwell*
HOW TO GET FABULOUSLY RICH, *Thomas Rockwell*
CHOCOLATE FEVER, *Robert Kimmel Smith*
BOBBY BASEBALL, *Robert Kimmel Smith*
IT'S A WEIRD, WEIRD SCHOOL, *Stephen Mooser*
THE HITCHHIKING VAMPIRE, *Stephen Mooser*

YEARLING BOOKS/YOUNG YEARLINGS/YEARLING CLASSICS are designed especially to entertain and enlighten young people. Patricia Reilly Giff, consultant to this series, received her bachelor's degree from Marymount College and a master's degree in history from St. John's University. She holds a Professional Diploma in Reading and a Doctorate of Humane Letters from Hofstra University. She was a teacher and reading consultant for many years, and is the author of numerous books for young readers.

For a complete listing of all Yearling titles,
write to Dell Readers Service,
P.O. Box 1045,
South Holland, IL 60473.

Gary Paulsen

Dunc and the Scam Artists

A YEARLING BOOK

Published by
Dell Publishing
a division of
Bantam Doubleday Dell Publishing Group, Inc.
666 Fifth Avenue
New York, New York 10103

ISBN: 0-440-40775-3

Printed in the United States of America

April 1993

10 9 8 7 6 5 4 3 2 1

OPM

Dunc and the Scam Artists

Chapter · 1

Duncan—Dunc—Culpepper sat on the living-room floor in his best friend for life's house, Amos.

Amos had baby-sitting duty today. His parents left him strict instructions. Visiting little cousins are human. No pounding, teasing, tormenting, name-calling, locking in the closet, or any other cruel or unusual punishment. They had taped a list to the refrigerator door. It was two pages of things Amos couldn't do to his baby cousin. Luckily, the list did not include making a play area by wrapping a volleyball

1

net around the dining-room table legs and keeping the baby in one spot that way.

Amos and Dunc were sitting on the living-room floor involved in a serious contest to determine who could stuff the most Oreo cookies inside his mouth without crunching them. Dunc had worked up to eleven but Amos was going for twelve when it happened.

The phone rang.

"It's her!" Amos yelled, or tried to yell. With twelve cookies in his mouth it came out, "Uuufffer!"

Instinct took over. It was probably not genetic codes—as Dunc thought—but for whatever reason, when Amos heard a phone ring, he assumed it was for him, assumed it was Melissa Hansen trying to call him, just him. Amos loved Melissa Hansen with all his heart, lived and died for Melissa Hansen and she didn't consider him at all. Ever.

But when the phone rang he couldn't help it. He had to answer it on the first ring, on that all-important first ring or he was afraid she would hang up. It didn't matter anymore that it was probably not Melissa—instinct had

taken over. When the phone rang, he moved.
And heaven help anybody in his way.

Dunc rolled sideways to get clear.

Amos came up in great form, powered by his
right leg, left leg kicking back hard. Reflex told
him where the nearest phone lay—exactly four
point three meters due east, on the lamp table
in the corner of the dining room.

He would have made it.

Even Dunc said later he would have made
it.

But he hung his right toe under the edge of
the couch. It didn't stay there—just hung for a
fraction of a second. But it was enough. His
body weight kept moving and he started down.

Even then he would have cleared it, perhaps
made the phone. But there was a goldfish bowl
on the end table by the couch and showing the
same classic form, he drove his head into the
bowl, cartwheeled just once—without spilling a
drop or killing the fish—and piled into the volleyball net under the table to land in a heap
next to his baby cousin.

The baby laughed and clapped his hands.

Dunc answered the phone, listened, said,
"No thank you," and hung up. "It was a sales-

person—they wanted to sell you a set of automobile manuals. I hope you didn't want them."

Amos signaled frantically for Dunc to pull the goldfish bowl off his head. He had opened his mouth and Oreo crumbs were filtering out. The goldfish were nibbling at them.

Dunc nodded and grabbed hold, then pulled the bowl off. Amos put the bowl back on the table and stood, brushing water and mushy Oreo pieces out of his hair. "I almost made it this time. Did you see how I corrected my forward body motion when I started to fall? I would have made it if the couch hadn't been there. Oh well, I'm glad she called, even if I didn't get to talk to her."

Dunc shook his head. "Didn't you hear me? It was a salesperson . . . well, never mind. It doesn't matter."

A car drove up outside and Amos nodded. "My folks. Maybe we'd better head on down to the mall before they get in here."

"But the baby."

"He'll be fine until they get in the house. That net will hold him."

"He's eating a goldfish."

"So? It's good protein. Come on."

4

Amos headed for the rear door. Dunc held back until Amos's parents were in the house before leaving the room just as the baby swallowed the fish.

Chapter · 2

"I can't go to the mall." They were riding down-town, lifting their front tires over cracks in the sidewalks. Dunc hit his brakes. "I just remem-bered. I told Dad I would deliver these real es-tate papers for him. Some lady wants a map cf the retirement village. It won't take long. Want to come?"

They turned around and pedaled their bikes across town and down a country lane on the west side. By the time they got to the house where the old lady lived, it was midafternoon.

"You didn't tell me we were going to go all the way to China," Amos shouted at Dunc, who had finally stopped up the road in front of an old rusty gate.

"We're here. I think. At least this is the address on the paper."

Amos looked past the gate to the old weather-beaten house. It stood at least two stories tall and was badly in need of a coat of paint. White curtains flapped in the open windows like dancing ghosts.

"It looks kinda spooky to me Dunc. I don't think anybody even lives here."

"Well, this is the address. Come on."

Dunc knocked on a front door that seemed ready to fall off its hinges. He was about to turn and leave when the door opened just a bit.

"What do you want?" a loud male voice boomed through the crack.

"We, ah—we are looking for the Dell house. These papers are for Mrs. Betsy Dell," stammered Dunc.

"I'll take those," the voice said.

"I was told to make sure and give them to Mrs. Dell personally."

The door slammed shut.

"Real friendly people your dad does business

8

with. Why didn't you just give the man the papers so we could get out of here?" Amos said.

"Don't you think that something's wrong here? That guy was pretty weird." Dunc wrinkled his eyebrows and stared at the house.

"Oh, no. I've seen that look before. Let's go before you get me into something we'll both regret."

"Let's just take a look around first. Then I promise we'll go." Dunc headed off the front porch and back around the side toward an old shed.

"Right." Amos sighed.

But he followed.

Chapter · 3

"Okay. Let's see what we've got," Dunc said in his most sleuthlike voice.

"We don't have anything," Amos said as he looked over his friend's shoulder at the list he was making. "Yesterday you found some soft dirt in an old lady's shed, with a shovel nearby. So what? It could be anything—we wouldn't have even gone in that shed if you hadn't been so nosy."

"Suspicious," Dunc corrected and scratched his head and looked up at Amos. "Doesn't it seem funny to you that we couldn't get past that creepy guy to see Mrs. Dell? On top of that, we find very fresh, soft dirt in the shed, where someone obviously buried something—or someone."

Amos shook his head. "No, it doesn't seem funny to me at all. Those things can both be easily explained. Besides, if you're really all that concerned, why don't you just call the police and let them check it out?"

"We need to tie it all together so we have enough evidence to nab the creep."

"Stop talking like that. I've told you before, you watch too many cop shows."

"Look Amos, I told my dad. He wasn't concerned. I don't think the cops will be either—yet."

"I can understand that. I'm not concerned and I've been in on it right from the start. Come on, let's go down to the river or play video games or something normal for a change."

Dunc wasn't paying any attention. He was thinking out loud. "What we need is a plan. We could scale the wall and climb in a top-story window. Or maybe we could learn karate and take the guy out."

Amos shook his head. His friend's crazy ideas were nothing new, but this time he had his mind made up. Nothing could make him get involved in this. Not even an army could force him to take on that guy who had yelled through the crack in the door. If there was something weird going on out there, he was certainly not going to be involved in it. No way.

Dunc had that strange look on his face. "I think I know how to do it. It won't be hard at all. In fact, you'll probably enjoy your part."

"You never listen to me Duncan Culpepper."

Dunc put his hand on his friend's shoulder. "I always listen to you. Didn't I help you get a good grade in Trasky's class on your Civil War paper? Don't I always try to help you get Melissa to notice you, even though she'd rather you would drop dead? Listening is one of my best points. I just need your cooperation in one tiny little area and after that we're home free."

Amos eyed him suspiciously. "I know I'm going to be sorry for asking you this, but what exactly do you have in mind?"

"I was hoping you'd ask. We have to get inside that house and look around."

Amos shook his head. "I'm not dressing up like a girl again, so just forget that."

"No, no, nothing like that. One of us will

13

have to distract the creep inside while the other one sneaks around back."

"Let me just guess who gets to take on the creep."

"I *would* do it Amos, really I would, but he's already seen me. Besides, I'm only trying to help you."

"Help me? How do you figure that?"

"Well, if this deal works out, like I'm sure it will, you're going to play the most important part in rescuing a helpless little old lady from who knows what awful fate. Some girls really go for the hero type."

"Some girls . . ."

"Melissa. Maybe."

"Melissa . . ."

Dunc stopped then. He knew when he'd won.

Chapter · 4

"Do you remember what you're going to do?"

"Of course I remember. How could anybody dressed like this forget what they're supposed to do?"

Dunc looked his friend up and down. Amos was wearing a red jacket with a double row of black buttons down the front. On his head was a round red hat with black elastic holding it on under his chin. "I think you really look the part, but try to be careful with the hat and coat, okay? I borrowed them from Melissa Hansen's mother. Her cousin used to do this for a living."

"Melissa Hansen? You saw Melissa?"

"Just for a second. I remembered her mother telling my mother that she had a cousin who delivered singing telegrams, so I borrowed the suit. Roll up the sleeves a little."

"You went to *Melissa's* house without me?"

"I had to borrow the suit Amos. Don't worry, maybe you can help me take it back. Let's get down to business. Why don't you practice your part one more time, okay?"

"Man, I can't believe you actually went to her house and didn't tell me . . ."

"Amos, pay attention. Let's practice your part."

"What did she say? Did she ask about me at all?"

"No, but I really wasn't there all that long. Are you going to practice or what?"

"Okay, but only if you give me your solemn promise to let me take the suit back with you. Promise?"

"I promise. Now, do your part."

"Dunc, I really don't sing so hot. Can't I just talk the guy a message?"

"No. We've been over and over this. Nobody interrupts a singer until he's through. So just keep singing while I make my way around back

16

and look for Mrs. Dell. Now come on. You have to practice."

"Here goes nothing," Amos shrugged.

> Singing telegram for Mrs. Dell
> Here it is clear as a bell:
> We wish you a happy day
> Because that is just our way.
> On this day have lots of fun.

A strange look came into Amos's eyes. He smiled, threw his arms out to the side and started to really get into the singing.

> Spend some time out in the sun,
> Open presents and eat cake,
> Take a trip down to the lake,
> Above all else, have a good time
> Hope you like our little rhyme.

Amos wound up on one knee on the floor, his hands out, a happy smile on his face.

Dunc stared at him. "Ahh—that's great Amos. Try to work on that shyness a little, all right?"

"How was the delivery?"

Dunc nodded. "Great. Great delivery."

"Good. I want to give it my best, you know."

It took the boys forty-five minutes to get across town to the Dell place. The rusty gate creaked as the boys went through.

Dunc hid across from the house in the weeds beside the shed as Amos cautiously approached the house. He knocked on the front door. No answer. He started off the porch and the door opened.

"May I help you young man?" It was a sweet elderly voice, and a small, elderly woman opened the door.

Amos looked at the little old lady in front of him. "I—that is, I—are you Mrs. Dell?"

"Why yes, dear. What can I do for you?"

"You can't do much for me, but I have a friend you can sure straighten out."

Amos waved wildly at Dunc.

Dunc came out of the bushes and walked up onto the porch. "Mrs. Dell?"

"Yes, I'm Mrs. Dell. What's going on here boys?"

Dunc explained about his last trip out to her house and about the strange man at the door and everything.

"You boys look tired. Come in the house. Let me get you some lemonade and we'll visit."

They were ushered into the living room and were served cookies and homemade lemonade. They sat on an overstuffed couch while the woman spoke to them.

"You see boys, that was my nephew Frank. Sometimes he's a little bit overprotective. I really appreciate your concern, though."

"Are you satisfied now?" Amos asked as they pushed their bikes through the old gate and headed back down the dirt road.

Dunc started to answer, but a little black poodle ran up to him, wiggling and waggling its tail.

"Where did you come from boy?" Dunc pulled his bike over to the side of the road.

"He's my baby boys. His name is Napoleon."

A gray-haired lady wearing an old, tattered straw hat with a dozen different kinds of flowers on it came from the side of the road, reached down and picked up the dog. She was holding a shovel in one hand and had obviously been working in her yard.

"My name is Cora Hawkins. Some folks call me Crazy Cora Hawkins. I don't mind. I live

19

right up the road. I saw you boys coming out of that thieves' hideout. Are you part of the gang?"

Dunc pointed at Amos. "He delivers telegrams and I'm just along for the ride. What makes you think there's a gang in that old house?" Dunc asked.

The old lady grinned. Two of her front teeth were missing. She shook her head and turned and walked away.

"They're up to no good over there. No good I tell you," she mumbled over her shoulder.

Chapter · 5

"It's really not fair," Amos said. "She didn't even look at me. The only thing she said was, 'Thanks for returning the suit.' I think she was talking to you."

"Cut it out Amos. I'm sure she noticed you. You tripped over her dog and fell into her rose bushes and almost killed her cat. She had to notice you."

The boys were in Dunc's bedroom cutting out newspaper clippings for a current events project.

Dunc read one headline out loud: " 'Elderly Taken In By Con Artist.' Look at this. Some guy posing as a long-lost relative convinces these old people to sign over all their property and bank accounts to him. Maybe we ought to look—"

Amos held up both hands. "Hold it right there. Look at the way the last deal you got me into turned out. You had me dress up in a monkey suit because you thought some lady was buried out in a shed or something."

"I never said she was buried in the shed. But something sure was. Listen to the description of this guy. He's unusually tall, has dark hair and a mustache. It sounds just like him."

"Like who?"

"Him. You know—the creep in the house."

"Come off it Dunc. You never even really saw him. You only heard his voice. Don't tell me you know what he looks like from a voice."

"Well, I'm pretty sure he was tall and I'm almost positive I saw a mustache. It could be him. We'd better check it out just in case."

As they rode their bikes to the retirement village, Amos pulled up close to Dunc. "How do I let you talk me into these things? I'm hungry, I'm tired, and this is a waste of time."

"It won't hurt to talk to these people and

when we get through we'll go over to Poncho's Pizza Palace—my treat."

Dunc pulled out a list of retirement village residents who had been taken in, that he had cut out of the newspaper. The first lady on the list was very nice but really did not remember a lot. She kept asking the boys their names. She thought they were selling magazine subscriptions.

But the next man remembered the con artist. He had driven a blue car, he said—but then again, it might have been brown.

After that, every resident they talked to said one thing that was the same: The crook had gotten away with their life savings and property or the investments they had made. He had always told them he was their great-grandson, nephew, or close family friend.

The police didn't have any leads—this guy was smooth. They knew he worked with a partner but no one had any idea who the unseen accomplice was.

Dunc and Amos rode in silence to the pizza place. Dunc was still immersed in thought while he was eating but Amos was really getting into his pizza. He had sauce in his hair, on his nose, and all over his face, down his shirt, in his lap, and on his hands up to his elbows.

They were just about to polish off an entire Poncho's Big Blob—about like eating a cheese-covered Buick—when a group of girls walked past their table.

"Melissa," Dunc said, looking up. "Nice to see you."

Melissa paused, smiled at Dunc, then looked down at Amos—covered in sauce and cheese. She turned and walked away.

"I guess she didn't know you." Dunc watched the girls go over to the video games. "Look Amos, there has to be a way to catch this guy. We can't just let him get away with it."

"That's probably it," Amos said.

"What?"

"She probably didn't see me because of the sauce and cheese. She won't know it was me."

"Amos, we've got more important stuff to worry about."

"Maybe I ought to clean up and go over there and try again."

"No Amos, I think you've impressed her enough for one day."

"What do you mean by that?"

"Nothing. I figure she saw you finishing that Big Blob. Not too many guys can handle one of those."

"Do you really think so? I could order another one—"

"Come on Amos, we've got work to do."

Chapter · 6

Dunc paced up and down the sidewalk in front of his house. He racked his brain, but for once a solution did not present itself.

"Will you stop it?" Amos yawned. "You're making me tired. You're not going to get anywhere on this one. You don't even have a case. And if you did, you don't have any proof. Besides, if we don't get finished with that current events assignment, we'll both be in hot water."

"That's it Amos! You're a genius."

"Don't tell me—you've come up with a plan involving me and hot water."

"No Amos. Don't you get it? Proof. We need proof. Why didn't I think of this before? I know ere the proof is. It's buried in Mrs. Dell's shed. The creep is posing as her nephew and using her place to hide from the cops. He's buried the evidence in the dirt floor of the shed."

"Right, and we'll just casually walk up to the door and ask to dig holes all over the poor woman's shed."

"Use your head Amos. We'll have to do it at night, when they're all asleep. I'll meet you at the usual place when you're all clear."

At midnight it was darker than usual. Both boys were waiting just outside the gate in front of Betsy Dell's house.

"Everyone is asleep," Dunc whispered.

"How can you be sure they're asleep?" Amos asked. "Do you always go to sleep at the stroke of midnight? My uncle Alfred, the one who picks his toes, he never goes to sleep at night. He sleeps in the daytime, sitting in front of the TV."

"I don't see any lights on in the house. We'd better go ahead and do it now whether they're asleep or not. If we don't we won't get back on time."

They left their bikes near the fence and

climbed over the squeaky gate so that it wouldn't groan and attract attention.

They were dressed in the black clothes and ski masks they always wore for special night missions.

Step by step they silently worked their way to the shed.

"You start digging and I'll keep a lookout," Dunc said.

"Naturally," Amos murmured. "Hey, where's the shovel? Shine your light over here. I thought it was right here."

"It was. Let's look around for it."

"It's not here now, so I guess we'll have to go home and forget all about it, right?" Amos was hopeful.

"We'll just have to use our hands. Start digging. I'll help you."

They scooped the dirt out with their bare hands.

"I've found something Dunc. Turn on your flashlight."

The light caught the top of a green metal box with a white handle in the shape of an angel.

"Let's see if we can get the rest of it uncovered," Dunc said.

The screen door on the front porch slammed shut. A tall figure walked out onto the porch and lit a cigarette.

The boys froze.

Dunc whispered softly, "Help me cover up the box and then get up against the wall. We'll watch out the window. If he comes this way, we'll have to make a run for it."

Amos nodded.

A second figure walked out onto the porch but it was too dark to tell much about it. They were too far away to make out what was being said.

". . . won't be long . . . enough money . . . retire . . . after . . . one . . . more . . . job . . ."

The boys inched toward the door of the shed. Suddenly the doorknob turned and an extremely large person walked into the shed. It was the creep.

"Where's the light switch? I can't see a thing in here," the big man said. He felt around and grabbed Amos by the ear.

"Run!" Amos screeched.

They ran wide open, out the door of the

shed, right over the big man. He went down, *whumping* up a cloud of dust.

In the dark it was hard to tell which direction they were running. Then Amos's foot pounded down onto a rake—rakes seemed to wait for him—and it came up and hit him perfectly between the eyes.

"Rake!" he yelled. "I've been raked—"

"Keep quiet Amos, I think we've lost them."

"Easy for you to say." Amos held his nose.

Dunc took his belt off and handed one end of it to Amos. "Hold on. We've got to stay together. Come on."

The boys crashed through some thick brush and ran smack into a picket fence.

"Our bikes are along here somewhere. Hurry *up* Amos. Amos? Amos, where are you?"

"I'm stuck Dunc. Turn on the flashlight and help me."

Dunc pointed the light at Amos, whose head was jammed between two rails of the wooden fence.

"Quit fooling around Amos. They'll be here any second. Pull it out."

"I'm not fooling around—help me get it off."

Dunc grabbed the fence and heaved. Amos's

head didn't budge. "I can't move it. The whole section wobbled but your head doesn't seem to want to come loose."

"Pull," Amos said. "Pull hard."

Just then, Dunc heard noise in back of him and he grabbed in panic and heaved, felt something give, and took off for the bicycles, dragging Amos behind.

Chapter · 7

Amos had bright red ears and a purple goose egg between his eyes.

Dunc inspected the bruises more closely. "Did you have any trouble explaining your appearance to your parents?"

"I was kind of worried when my dad had to use the power saw to get that section of fence off of my head. I thought he might ask how it got there. But you know, he never did. He just kept mumbling something about how it wasn't fair how you couldn't pick your kids."

"I guess they're sort of used to your accidents by now," Dunc said.

"That's for sure. This morning my mom

looked right at me, fence and all, and asked me if I had slept well."

"Cheer up Amos. We came awful close to getting our case solved last night. Let's go up to my room and figure out where we went wrong."

"I can't. My uncle Alfred and my cousin, Little Brucie, are coming over after a while. My mom says I have to be home when the little monster arrives so that I can keep him from wrecking the place and eating the other goldfish. Besides, I know where I went wrong. It was when I agreed to go along with you last night. I should have stayed home and knitted."

"Can you knit Amos? I didn't know you could do that." The look spread across Dunc's face. "It just might come in handy sometime."

"Dunc, that is just an expression. Something people say when they wish they had stayed at home and minded their own business."

"You probably have all sorts of talent Amos. There's probably no limit to your abilities."

Amos rubbed the knot on his forehead. "If it's all the same to you, I'd rather leave my abilities untapped. By the way, we are going to leave this particular case alone now that we've tipped off the bad guys, aren't we?"

"Sure Amos, I just need to check into a couple of things and then we'll give it up. You go on over and watch Little Brucie. I need to go downtown for a while. When I get back, I'll come over and help you."

Without the volleyball net, Little Brucie was in rare form. From the time he arrived until Dunc got back from town, he led Amos on a wild chase, destroying anything that got in his path.

When Amos wasn't looking, he superglued Amos's new tennis shoes to the bathroom floor. While he was in the bathroom, he stuffed seven rolls of toilet paper down the toilet and when Amos caught up with him, he was crawling after the cat with a hair dryer in one hand.

Dunc yelled as he rode up the driveway, "Amos, come down here. I've got news for you."

"You come up here. I can't take my eyes off this kid for one minute. He's liable to torch the place."

Dunc walked in the front door and ducked just in time to avoid a flying bowl of red Jell-O.

"Hey, what's going on here?"

"Brucie is playing flying saucer," Amos said.

"Cute kid."

"I've had enough fun for one day. I'm going to get my mom to watch this little alien."

Securely out of Little Brucie's reach, the boys relaxed in Dunc's room.

"So what big news do you have for me?" Amos asked.

"Well, I checked on Mrs. Dell's property. It hasn't been stolen. I also found out that she hasn't reported being robbed or anything."

"That's nice for her. So what's the big deal?"

"Don't you get it Amos? The crooks haven't made their play yet. We still may have time to save her."

"Dunc, I don't think you live in the real world with the rest of us. What do you think we are, a couple of superheroes or something?"

"No really Amos—I have a plan that might just save Mrs. Dell and catch the crooks at the same time."

"You always have a plan. That's the trouble. But they never work out the way you plan them."

"This one is so simple, it's got to work. Listen, I already talked to Mrs. Dell and set it up without her really knowing about it."

Chapter · 8

It was a superhot day, one of those days when Amos thought he'd like to just live inside the air conditioner.

But instead, Amos was sweating and complaining. "Why did your plan have to involve physical labor? You didn't have to tell her we were Boy Scouts trying to earn a merit badge. At least we could have gotten paid. This is our one and only spring break. It only lasts two weeks and then it's gone."

"A little yard work never hurt anybody Amos. I've been noticing your arms lately."

"What's wrong with my arms?"

"They're kinda puny. They could be a little more solid, have a little more muscle."

"I really don't care if I ever have any muscles or not, especially if this is the way you get them," Amos said tiredly.

Dunc chopped another weed. "Well, you know I don't care, but some girls like guys with muscles."

Amos dropped his rake and stood up as straight as he could. He puffed out his chest and flexed his skinny arms. Then shook his head. "Melissa will have to love me like I am—I think it's hopeless. Let's leave and go eat more pizza."

"Maybe later. Right now, we need to stay here and watch the house. If the creep comes back, we've got to stop him from scamming Mrs. Dell."

They worked steadily in the hot sun all day. But absolutely nothing unusual happened—except for the time Amos used the electric weed-walloper and it got away from him. Luckily, the motor ran out of gas before it took all of Amos's hair off, but it did leave him looking patchy and his ears were welted. Mrs. Dell brought them some lemonade to drink with their lunch and some cookies for a snack in the afternoon and she made a point of not staring at Amos. Between the weed-walloper and the picket fence, he looked as if he'd tried to kiss a rotary mower.

The front yard looked great and the mountain of weeds by the shed was gone.

While they worked near the shed, they took the opportunity to look around. This time Amos had guard duty while Dunc searched. He dug in the exact spot where Amos had found the green metal box. Nothing was there.

The only clues the crooks had left were large footprints and those could have been left at any time.

"What a bust," Amos said as they wearily pedaled for home.

"Maybe something will turn up tomorrow." Dunc sighed.

The next morning started off the same way. The boys mowed the grass in the back yard and kept an eye out for anything suspicious.

About two o'clock a blue, late-model car pulled up in Mrs. Dell's driveway. A large man got out and walked into the house without knocking.

Dunc moved close to the living-room window and peered in to get a better look. "It's him—I knew it. He's got a mustache and everything. Look Amos, he's got some papers. He probably wants her to sign something. We've got to get closer so we can hear."

They crawled around to the front porch. The door was wide open.

The big man was talking, "Look, I said I had some important business to discuss with you."

"Now Frank dear, I told you not to come back here. You shouldn't be here."

Dunc grabbed Amos by the shoulder. "Quick, we gotta think of something. We can't let him get her to sign anything. Go ask for a drink of water."

Before he had time to think, Amos knocked on the door and shouted, "Mrs. Dell, I hate to bother you, but could I have a drink of water?"

"Who's that?" the big man asked gruffly.

"Just a sweet boy who's volunteered to do some yard work for me." Mrs. Dell called to the front door. "Come in dear. Go right on in to the kitchen and get your drink. The glasses are on the drainboard."

The man growled, "Are you out of your mind? We don't need anybody around here, least of all now. You get rid of that kid. I mean it. We've got business to take care of—urgent business."

Amos took his time in the kitchen. First he got a drink. Then he washed his hands. Then he blew his nose loudly on a paper towel.

"That is a real nice kitchen you've got there Mrs. Dell," he said, walking back into the living room. "In fact, you have a real nice place here. The water tastes great too. Thanks."

Amos stood in the living room looking around and making small talk. "Is this your nephew? Nice to meet you. Do you live around here?"

"Hrummp." The big man brushed Amos aside and strode out the front door. "I'll be back and you'd better be ready to talk business."

Dunc made it around the corner of the house just in time to remain unseen.

"Thanks again for the water. I'd better be going." Amos moved to the door.

Outside, Dunc beamed at Amos. "You were

great. I didn't know you had it in you. You saved the day."

Amos thought about it, then nodded. "I was kind of great, wasn't I?"

Chapter·9

Tragedy struck.

Little Brucie had exposed Amos to the chicken pox.

Amos looked awful. Small red bumps covered his entire body. White sticky lotion covered the red bumps. Between weed-wallopers, picket fences and now chicken pox, he looked like the original leper.

"How come you never had this stuff when you were a kid?" Dunc asked. "I think I got 'em when I was about five."

"Just lucky I guess," Amos replied sullenly. "What are we gonna do about the case now?"

"Don't worry about it. You just relax and try

not to itch. I rode out to Mrs. Dell's place to see if she had any more work for us. There was a note on the door. She's going out of town for a while. So she'll be okay and we can just take it easy. Do you want anything?"

"Yeah—Little Brucie's head on a platter."

"Seriously. I brought you all kinds of snacks and comics and junk. All guaranteed to make you feel better."

"Hand over one of those Elastic Man comics. What are you going to do with the rest of your spring break?"

"I guess we better keep trying to think of a way to get the goods on the creep before he rips off somebody else. By the way, did you see that new piece in the paper about the old folks who were already ripped off? The article says the police think the crooks have probably left town. We may never see them again."

"That wouldn't break my heart. Besides, I thought you were going to stay here and take care of me in my hour of need." Amos pouted. "You know, bring me pizza, and . . ."

"I am. I am—mostly. I just thought if we needed something to do, we could think about it."

"You go right ahead, Dunc. Give it your best shot. Think up your wildest, most off-the-wall plan. Just remember—I'm sick."

"Well, I was thinking about having you dress up like an old woman, since you can knit and all, and trying to lure the crooks back here. I thought you could—"

"Boy, am I glad I'm sick. Maybe Brucie's not such a bad kid after all."

"Don't worry. I knew that one wouldn't work. You don't have anything a crook would want—that is, besides your baseball cards. And I'm not sure the crooks would come all the way back here for a four-dollar-and-seventy-five-cent baseball card collection."

Amos wasn't paying attention. He had backed up to the closet and was rubbing his backside up and down against the edge of the door.

"Stop that," Dunc ordered. "Do you want all those bumps to turn inside out and make gross, ugly marks all over you? Your mom said not to scratch. Get back in bed and behave yourself."

"I can't help it. This is worse than that time when we were running from a bear and I fell in the poison ivy."

"It wasn't a bear. It was Carley's little brother in his Roy Raccoon suit. And you wouldn't have fallen if you hadn't gotten so scared that you tied your shoelaces together in a hurry to get dressed."

"Details," Amos said. "Anyway, this is worse."

"Try not to think about it. Look at the bright side. You are going to be well in time for Melissa's birthday party."

"Melissa's having a birthday party? How do you know? No one told me about it."

"Her mother told mine. They're in the same bowling league. Anyway, that's a long time from now. You ought to be as good as new by then."

Amos had a worried look on his face. "I bet she's been calling and calling me. And I'm stuck up here in bed, not even allowed to come downstairs so I won't infect anybody else. I wonder if I could get a phone installed up here in my room?"

Dunc threw a pillow at him. "I wish I had never mentioned it. I just thought it would make you happy to know that you'll be well by then."

"Happy? I've got to start making plans for a fabulous present. Something that will really wow her. Diamonds would probably be a little much. What about a sports car? A red one with a sun roof?"

"Amos, she can't drive yet. Get real. I have to go now. I'll come over and check on you tomorrow."

Chapter · 10

Amos was staring at himself in the mirror above Dunc's dresser.

"I think they are all gone. I can't find any bumps anywhere."

"Too bad you were sick most of spring break. Pure bad luck, having to go back to school on the first day you're well," Dunc said.

"You said it. Trasky really poured on the homework too. He thinks all we have to do at night is sit around reading about Attila the Hun."

Dunc picked up a folder from the dresser. "Mrs. Ellerthorp gave me an A on my current events project about the elderly. She hopes they catch the crooks."

"She gave me a C. Just because I dropped it in Scruff's water dish. You could still read it and everything. It was just slightly wrinkled. Some people are overly picky," Amos said.

Dunc was looking at his paper. "Want to ride over and check on Mrs. Dell before we get started on our homework? She could be back from vacation by now. I'd like to make sure that her so-called nephew isn't busy trying to pull a fast one on her."

"You've got my vote. Anything beats homework. Hey, let's stop and get a triple-whammy grape Sno-Kone on our way."

Mrs. Hawkins waved at them as they rode past her house. She held Napoleon, the poodle, in her lap the way you would hold a real baby.

At Mrs. Dell's house, no one was home. They decided to sit on the front porch and finish what was left of their Sno-Kones before heading back.

Then a strange scratching sound came from inside the house.

"Did you hear that?" Dunc asked.

Amos gulped. "Yeah, I heard it. It's coming from just inside that door. It's the same sound the monsters make in movies. The kind where they eat people."

Dunc walked over to the door and slowly opened it. A ball of black fur jumped into his face.

"Meeooww."

A large black cat ran off into the bushes.

Amos laughed. "That cat sure had me worried for a minute."

Dunc didn't hear a word he said. He was staring transfixed into the living room.

"What is it?" Amos said. "Is something wrong? What are you looking at?"

Dunc pointed toward the doorway.

Amos ran over to the door, spilling what was left of his Sno-Kone down the front of his shirt.

Across the room, sitting on a low table, was a green metal box with a white handle in the shape of an angel.

Chapter · 11

"What is that doing here?" Amos said.

"We have a situation," Dunc said. "I think the crooks are back. Poor Mrs. Dell is probably in a lot of trouble. We'd better get that box down to the police station."

Amos picked up the box. "This thing weighs a ton. What's in here?"

Carefully, he opened the lid.

Money.

Stacks of money.

"Wow, I've never seen so much money in all my life." Amos said.

"Here's the evidence we need." Dunc pulled several titles and bank books out of the box.

"How do you suggest we carry this thing on our bikes all the way downtown?" Amos asked.

"Look around for a stick or something we can run under the handle. We'll ride carrying it between us on a pole." He looked quickly around the room and shook his head. "There's nothing that will work in here. I'll get something from the shed."

He had just stepped inside the tool shed when he heard a car pull up. He saw the creep and Mrs. Dell get out and go inside the house.

Dunc watched helplessly from the shed window. Amos was in there alone.

He tried to clear his thoughts.

He had to come up with a surefire way to get Amos out of there.

He had to do something.

What?

He frowned. Maybe it wasn't as bad as he thought it was. Maybe Amos had heard them drive up and had hidden. Maybe the creep wouldn't catch him after all. It was possible that they wouldn't even know Amos was in there. He and Dunc had parked their bikes at the side of the house, after all.

They probably didn't suspect a thing, Dunc decided.

I'll just wait right here. They'll have to go somewhere after a while and then Amos will be free to come out of hiding.

Time ticked by slowly, seeming to drag along, making Dunc feel impossibly old.

How long should he wait? What if the creep had caught Amos? He could be torturing him for information even now. Rubbing honey on him and looking around for an anthill.

Dunc shook all over. That was it. He couldn't wait any longer. Amos was his best friend. No matter what happened, Dunc had to try and save him.

He looked around the shed for something that would take the creep's attention off of Amos. An ax handle was leaning against the back wall.

He grabbed the handle and ran for the door.

A blue car was parked in front of the house. Dunc eased up behind it and slipped around to the driver's side.

The door made an irritating metallic screech as he opened it.

He held his breath. No one came out of the house.

Dunc took the ax handle and propped it up in the driver's seat. Then he took a deep breath and quickly wedged it against the car's horn.

Hoonnnnnkkk!

Dunc ran wide open for the back door and slammed around the corner, just as the front door flew open and the creep ran out to his car.

Amos came flying out the back door at the same time and nearly ran over Dunc.

"No time to explain," Dunc said. "We've got to hide. He'll be looking for us. Under the back porch. *Now!*"

Chapter · 12

The creep was talking to someone: "There are two of them. They're still here somewhere. I found two bikes by the side of the house. You look in the house and I'll check down by the creek."

It was pitch black under the old wooden porch. Amos tried not to breathe. Something had definitely died under there recently. The smell was almost unbearable. The stale ground was rocky and uncomfortable.

Amos felt something crawling up the back of his shirt. He couldn't reach it and it was driving him crazy. He tried to ignore it and had almost succeeded—when he remembered centipedes.

He'd seen them in *National Geographic*. They bit you. They had poison. They could kill you. First things fell off and then you died.

It was too much. Amos exploded out from under the porch as if he'd been fired from a missile launcher. Dunc grabbed for him, missed, and called after him in a loud whisper. "Amos—get back in here before you get caught."

"Too late for that boys. You're caught," the big man boomed.

A flashlight beamed at Dunc under the porch.

"Come out of there squirt."

Dunc crawled out and stood up. "We were just inspecting the structure of the house. Pretty weak supports under the porch, if you ask me."

"Shut up and get in the house. Don't try anything or I'll tie your arms and legs in knots."

Oh great, Dunc thought. *Another plan bites the dust.*

The big man shoved them toward the couch.
"Sit down."

Mrs. Dell came down the stairs.

"Oh, dear. What's going on here?"

Dunc turned to the lady. "Mrs. Dell you've
got to help us. This is a bad man. He isn't your
nephew. He has us here against our will. We
think he may be trying to steal from you.
Please call the police."

She smiled at him like a kind aunt or grand-
mother. "Of course Frankie is my nephew,
dear. I've known him since he was a little boy. I
don't think you understand. Frankie and I
work together on little projects. I only let you
boys work here to throw you off our trail. I'm
afraid it didn't work, did it?"

"I told you not to let them hang around here.
You should have let me take care of them,"
Frankie almost snarled.

The look on Mrs. Dell's face became hard.
"Shut up Frankie. Without me, you'd be nothing. You'd still be stealing hubcaps in L.A."

Dunc's mouth fell open. "You mean you're
both crooks? You are the partner the police
have been looking for?"

"Pretty good disguise, isn't it?" said Mrs.

Dell in her sweetest grannylike voice. "You see, Frankie here does all the inside work, but I introduce him to the pigeons. Older people seem to trust older people. They really shouldn't you know. We can be bad just as well as good."

Amos shook his head. "I can't believe a nice lady like you would be involved in something as dishonest as this. You should be ashamed of yourself."

"Now, now, don't get excited honey. Everybody has to make a living."

"That's enough talk," Frankie said. "What should I do with them Auntie?"

Mrs. Dell's sweet expression changed again. "Take them upstairs and lock them in a closet. By the time they get out, we'll be in sunny Mexico."

Frankie marched them upstairs and shoved them into a small closet.

"Can't we talk about this?" Amos asked.

Frankie slammed the door in his face.

"Not very talkative, is he?"

Dunc pushed on the door. "Gorillas don't have a very good command of the English language."

The closet was dark, too dark to see anything. There was only enough room to stand up or sit with their knees pulled up close.

This was going from bad to worse, Dunc thought. Out loud he said, "Don't worry Amos. I'll think of something."

"You mean, this was not a part of your original plan?" Amos's voice was sarcastic.

"Not exactly. It's more like a sidetrack. But I'm sure something will turn up."

Amos sighed. "I sure hope it does soon. It's getting hard to breathe in here."

He had no sooner said that than they began to hear sirens. Police sirens.

"Here comes the cavalry," Dunc said. "Let's let them know where we are."

They pounded and kicked the closet door and screamed at the top of their lungs.

"Stand back from the door. We'll have to pry it open."

The door flew open and two grateful boys came tumbling out to land at the feet of two policemen.

"Thanks officers," Dunc said.

"No problem. We heard the racket and figured someone was in here."

Downstairs, two officers were sorting

61

through the green metal box. Handcuffs were being applied to Mrs. Dell, who was protesting and claiming her innocence in her sweetest little-old-lady voice.

"Good work boys." The officer in charge shook their hands. "We've been after these two for a long time."

Out in the yard the creep was facedown in the grass. His arms were outstretched, and his knees were bent and his feet were sticking straight into the air.

"What happened to him?" Amos asked.

"I did." Mrs. Hawkins came up from the side of the porch. "I saw you two ride in, but I never saw you ride out. So I called the police, then came over on my own to check things out. He came after me and I hit him."

"Hit him?" Dunc asked. "What with?"

"A shovel. It left a print of his face in the metal. I hate to ruin a good shovel like that but it was an emergency."

"Well, however it worked out, thank you for saving us. We might have been in that closet for years." Dunc smiled. "If there's anything we can do for you, just let us know."

Mrs. Hawkins studied him. "To be honest, I

could use a couple of strong boys to do a little yard work over at my place."

Amos shook his head, tried to signal Dunc but it didn't work.

"You've got it," Dunc said.

Chapter · 13

The police were kind enough to take the two exhausted boys and their bikes home.

Dunc's parents restricted him to the house, Mrs. Hawkins's yard, and school until further notice or old age, whichever came first. Amos's parents hadn't even missed him, except that the house didn't seem to be quite as wrecked as usual, so he could go over to Dunc's house.

Dunc was sitting on his bed. "We're getting pretty good at this detective stuff. I think I'll work us up a resume. Maybe we should advertise. All things considered, I think this was one of our better cases, don't you?"

"If you like centipedes, dark closets, the Incredible Hulk pushing you around and your life being threatened, I guess it was great." Amos said. "Personally, I'd rather have a tooth pulled."

"Every case has its drawbacks. It's the end result that matters. Mrs. Dell and her nephew are in custody. Frankie is squealing like a stuck pig. The police have enough evidence to put them both away for a long time. It's a great feeling knowing we were a part of it."

"Too bad the newspapers don't feel the same way. They didn't even mention us in the article. The police got all the credit."

Dunc shrugged. "Oh well, that's one of the things you have to expect when you're a detective. We do all the work and they get all the glory."

"I was counting on some of that glory. Remember? Melissa was supposed to want my autograph."

"I know it didn't quite work out that way this time. But don't worry—there's always next time."

"Count me out. I've had enough cops and robbers for one lifetime," Amos said.

"Speaking of Melissa, have you gotten an invitation to her party yet?" Dunc asked. "It's only two days away."

"You don't have to remind me. I've been ready for two weeks. My invitation probably got lost in the mail. Either that, or she wants to call and invite me personally."

The phone chose that exact moment to ring.

Dunc tried to stop him. "Amos, it's not her. This is my phone, remember? She wouldn't call you here."

But by that time the back screen door was off its hinges, the garbage cans were flying through the yard, the rear fence was flattened and Amos was hanging in Mrs. Elmore's clothesline across the alley.

"Amos, are you alive?"

A hand waved weakly at him through the clothesline ropes.

Dunc sighed and went for a pair of scissors to cut Amos loose.

It was going to be a long school year.

Be sure to join Dunc and Amos in these other Culpepper Adventures:

The Case of the Dirty Bird

When Dunc Culpepper and his best friend, Amos, first see the parrot in a pet store, they're not impressed—it's smelly, scruffy, and missing half its feathers. They're only slightly impressed when they learn that the parrot speaks four languages, has outlived ten of its owners, and is probably 150 years old. But when the bird starts mouthing off about buried treasure, Dunc and Amos get pretty excited—let the amateur sleuthing begin!

Dunc's Doll

Dunc and his accident-prone friend, Amos, are up to their old sleuthing habits once again. This time they're after a band of doll thieves! When a doll that once belonged to Charles Dickens's daughter is stolen from an exhibition at the local mall, the two boys put on their detective gear and do some serious snooping. Will a vicious watchdog keep them from retrieving the valuable missing doll?

Culpepper's Cannon

Dunc and Amos are researching the Civil War cannon that stands in the town square when they find a note inside telling them about a time portal. Entering it through the dressing room of La Petite, a women's clothing store, the boys find themselves in downtown Chatham on March 8, 1862—the day before the historic clash between the *Monitor* and the *Merrimack*. But the Confederate soldiers they meet mistake them for Yankee spies. Will they make it back to the future in one piece?

Dunc Gets Tweaked

Best friends Dunc and Amos meet up with a new buddy named Lash when they enter the radical world of skateboard competition. When somebody "cops"—steals—Lash's prototype skateboard, the boys are determined to get it back. After all, Lash is about to shoot for a totally rad world's record! Along the way they learn a major lesson: *Never* kiss a monkey!

Dunc's Halloween

Dunc and his best friend, Amos, are planning the best route to get the most candy on Halloween. But their plans change when Amos is slightly bitten by a werewolf. He begins scratching himself and chasing UPS trucks: he's become a werepuppy!

Dunc Breaks the Record

Best friends for life Dunc and Amos have a small problem when they try hang gliding—they crash in the wilderness. Luckily, Amos has read a book about a boy who survived in the wilderness for fifty-four days. Too bad Amos doesn't have a hatchet. Things go from bad to worse when a wild man holds the boys captive. Can anything save them now?

Dunc and the Flaming Ghost

Dunc's not afraid of ghosts, although Amos is sure that the old Rambridge house is haunted by the ghost of Blackbeard the Pirate. Then the best friends meet Eddie, a meek man who claims to be impersonating Blackbeard's ghost in order to live in the house in peace. But if that's true, why are flames shooting from his mouth?

Amos Gets Famous

Deciphering a code they find in a library book, best friends for life Amos and Dunc stumble onto a burglary ring. The burglars' next target is the home of Melissa, the girl of Amos's dreams (who doesn't even know that he's alive). Amos longs to be a hero to Melissa, so nothing will stop him from solving this case—not even a mind-boggling collision with a jock, a chimpanzee, and a toilet.

Dunc and Amos Hit the Big Top

In order to impress Melissa, the girl of his dreams, Amos decides to perform on the trapeze at the visiting circus. Look out below! But before his best friend for life, Dunc, can talk him out of his plan, the two stumble across a mystery behind the scenes at the circus. Now Amos is in double trouble. What's really going on under the big top?

Dunc's Dump

Camouflaged as piles of rotting trash, Dunc and Amos are sneaking around the town dump. Dunc wants to find out who is polluting the garbage at the dump with hazardous and toxic waste. Amos just wants to impress Melissa. Can either of them succeed?